ALSO BY JOSEPH CHAMBERLIN

Novella

Our Father Frank, The Story of a Priest, The Woman He Loved and The Sons They Left Behind, a novella based on the lives of his biological parents—a Roman Catholic priest and the married parishioner who sought his counsel.

Poetry

Life in the Breach and Other Poems

A Doctor Dies

and other stories

ELLE + KRIS ENJOY —

Joseph Chamberlin

4-19-13

A Doctor Dies and other stories

"Anticipation" was first published in the *Urbanite,* Baltimore, Maryland, July 2007

"Dad's Gift" was first published as "He Gave Us His World" in *The Washington Post,* December 1997

This book may be ordered through booksellers or by contacting *lulu.com.*

ISBN: 978-1-300-86828-6 (sc)

DEDICATED

TO

MY BROTHER

MICK

THOMAS MICHAEL CHAMBERLIN

HE HAS THE REST OF THE STORIES

THANK YOU

MARGARET OSBURN

FOR EDITING THESE STORIES

AND

KEVIN O'MALLEY

FOR DESIGNING THE COVER

CONTENTS

Footprints

SOUNDS OFTEN FRIGHTENED HIM and kept him restless as unquiet memories marched through his mind. This morning was different. Almost smiling, he sat himself up on the edge of the bed, reached for his jeans and managed to pull them over his new legs. He finished dressing himself with a red sweatshirt emblazoned Semper Fi and tried not to make too much noise as he moved himself into the kitchen. When he entered, his family's voices fell silent. The room filled with smiles.

     "Daddy. Daddy...you're up!"

IT WAS THE stillness of the newly fallen snow that had stirred him from bed. He'd opened his eyes to the morning brightness and lain there a moment to take in his wife's scent. It lingered on the warm print sheets, sheets so much more welcoming than those of the hospital bed where he'd spent so many months during the last year and a half. He had waited long for a morning such as this.

     The snow, the wonderful white of winter covered the world, his world—the world he had dreamed of as his sweat had soaked through the layers of clothing he'd worn over there in the desert. He was glad for the cold, grateful for the opportunity to struggle to prepare for this day, a day more than a few of his colleagues no longer had.

     Slowly, with a cadence he'd learned on drill fields, he'd moved what was left of his body to the edge of the bed, pausing only to take in the sweet sound of muffled voices, hers softening theirs with "Shh...Daddy's still asleep."

He knew the routine. He'd gotten past most of the dread some time ago. With the certainty of assembling his rifle, he'd lifted and affixed the one and then the other leg to the rounded cotton-covered remnants of his knees. He no longer experienced pain as much as awkwardness, which was also now finding a place in his life.

So, as he'd gone about the task of dressing, he'd remembered how he'd sworn he wouldn't do this. He wouldn't go through this. *Not me. No way. No how. I'd rather be dead...*

SHE WAS GLAD to be able to pour coffee into his favorite mug. He took a sip as he reached the counter and, looking at the three of them, said, "Well, what are you waiting for? Why aren't you all dressed? Time's a wastin'." With that, his son and daughter scurried from the room. And, within an instant, they were back.

The young boy struggled with his snow pants and one boot, while his older sister asked Mom for help with the gloves she hoped matched her jacket. Mom smiled as she helped the boy find his missing boot and gave approval of the girl's gloves. She made sure which hat belonged on whose head.

Dad watched, amazed, and was soon helping. Before long, he stood at the door, the cold trying to push into the house even before the door had been opened. Then, from the open doorway, the three stood looking out as if waiting for their portrait to be painted.

Outside, the carpet was winter white. He breathed in the crisp Saturday morning. The children looked to him as they always had. He would show them what to do. He took the first steps, stretched out one leg and placed it slowly, firmly into the fresh, undisturbed snow. And, as he placed his second foot to begin his third step, they stopped and turned. No one spoke a word. They smiled as they gazed at his footprints in the snow.

A Doctor Dies

THREE MONTHS AND IT was over.

"You don't really have to do this," she said.

"No. I want to help," he insisted.

So mother and son set about the task of removing the doctor's pajama bottoms and soiled diaper, cleaning him and dressing him in clean underwear and pajamas after the hospice nurse came and left. Then, as they sat waiting for the undertaker, the son's mood lightened. "You know, Mom, it's really icy out. Maybe we should put on his boots and jacket," said the boy, smiling.

THAT LAST WEEK had been full. The doctor told them it would not be long. As had become the custom, someone had stayed with them at the house most weekends—except that last one. A heavy snowfall on Friday night had kept everyone home.

Saturday she'd dressed her husband and began to make his breakfast. Noticing his eyes follow her around the room, she'd wheeled him close to the refrigerator and pointed. "Eggs? Do you want eggs?"

He didn't seem to want any particular thing—maybe he'd just wanted to be close to her.

After breakfast she'd taken him to his bed and propped him up so he could watch their son and daughter play in the snow. They'd made snowballs and thrown them against his window. He'd smiled.

Her joy had been in the watching. She'd savored every moment.

Two weeks before, the doctor had given her morphine patches to ease her husband's pain. Everyone had come that weekend. She'd brought him to the kitchen table, then returned him to his bed, and the family had sat and talked with her awhile.

AT ONE O'CLOCK that last morning, she'd told her daughter, "I want you to stay here with your dad." When she'd returned a few minutes later, she'd noticed a change in her husband's breathing. It seemed slower, less strained. "You have to call my sister," she'd told the girl.

"Why? It sounds as if he's resting."

"No. No! Call my sister," insisted the mother.

She sat close to her husband and listened to his breathing as her sister and niece joined with her and her son and daughter at his bedside. At last, he pulled himself up, seemed to look beyond them, his grimace replaced by a smile. She and her niece and her son would later describe the moment his head slumped back to his pillow as one in which they'd breathed a collective breath with his. He was gone.

HIS NAME WAS Paul. Dr. Paul. He'd been working as a scientist for years to find a cure for glioblastoma multiforme—glioblastoma, a brain tumor that kills in months was now killing him. He'd gone from being a vital, accomplished 46-year-old research scientist to being an "old baby," as his daughter described him.

As a scientist, Paul had known what it meant to be focused. He'd had the ability to attend to the most minute details but now that he was dying, his scientific work no longer seemed to matter. Inattentive, he was sent off to sit before his television.

It was Ann who talked with the doctors, deciding a battle plan, a plan conceived not to win, but to stave off the inevitable. The plan was to open his brain and take out whatever cancer they could. Chemo was an option, but not really a viable one. It would cost too much, take too many good cells, take too much of what was left of his diminishing life. The craniotomy, the opening of the brain, had more promise, a hope for more time, time which could be normal time; brain surgery might even allow him to drive a car.

But that was not to be. His time grew less and less and less. And less was his ability to be present, to look into Ann's eyes and to smile, to touch her in the middle of the night or early in the morning just before another day—when one day less began.

IN HER DREAMS they were normal. Once, as he'd lay in bed after a procedure, she'd fallen asleep. In a dream it was a bright, sunny morning and they were sitting across from one another, having coffee and talking as the kids watched TV in the other room. Then she awoke. "I want to go back to sleep!" she'd said to him.

AS SHE'D DONE what needed to be done, she'd wondered why no one had told her that caring for a dying man is like caring for a child. But that was not the most difficult. What was most difficult was not being able to converse with her husband. She could tell him about the day or about the beauty of the sunlight coming in through the windows or about the kids as they traversed from being children to young adults, but what was most difficult was the silence that followed the questions she continued to ask, knowing he was trying to answer.

Her own pain had worsened with each passing day, until one morning, after placing his arm on her side, she noticed him grimace. "What's the matter?" she asked and was surprised to hear him say, "We no longer exist."

"What do you mean?" she asked.

"This disease has separated us."

Later, in the middle of the night, she'd felt warmth, wonderful warmth. Not until she awoke did she realize he had lost control of his bladder. And then, there she was in the grocery store, in the middle of the night, watching them spray for bugs as she shopped for Depends.

HER MOST RECENT memories are of brushing Paul's teeth and soaking his radiation-burned scalp. But she has many memories. More and more, she will learn to rely upon these memories. Their wedding. She had waited years. *They* had waited. There was college and then his doctoral program to earn his PhD. Although it had taken them time to find their rhythm, they had.

At Paul's last birthday dinner they'd sat across from each other at the Princeton Sheraton sipping one more cocktail, the one that was more than enough. Then, in the parking lot, she'd slid her seat back and, in her coy way, "I have a present for you," asked him to do the same.

She was not wearing stockings and soon was without her panties. Slowly she moved, sliding over the car seat to his side, sliding up her dress to expose the top of her thigh, taking his hand to her bare skin as she pulled him closer. Kissing him, she reached over, unzipped his trousers and loosened his belt. She did not entertain a single thought about whether her actions might be visible or whether what she had started was opposite the law. Whatever was outside the car seemed farther and farther away as they moved closer and closer together until entwined, coming to enjoy one another in a way that was more sweet and satisfying than any birthday dessert, even chocolate. He had already begun to become the memory that would now sustain her.

.

Brian's Day

BARNEY IS WISHING HIS little friends a merry Christmas as the video ends and the viewer of the video, 13-year-old Brian, rolls off his ruffled bed that is speckled with photographs, a carry-out menu and last night's frozen pizza box to make his way across the scuff-proof floor, turn off the TV, pop out the video and neatly place it in a small plastic container along with the others. Softly singing, he strolls to the top of the steps, moving his head left to right. It is almost spring and Brian is about his day.

"Mom, Mom...Mom." He sits on the landing at the top of the stairs, like a not-so-small Buddha. He sits and calls for his mother who is downstairs in the living room kneeling before her Gohonzon, the place where she finds her strength.

"I hun'ry...Mom, Bry'n hun'ry."

"Come down here if you want to talk to me," she says, rising and walking into the kitchen.

"Bry'n hun'ry," he says again, crossing all imaginary lines that separate him from her. He is in her face, touching her arm. "Bry'n hun'ry," he repeats, looking about for something, anything to eat.

"Brian, stop. Remember personal space." She moves around him to pour herself a second cup of coffee.

"Keep han's to self," he responds.

"That's right."

With her cup of coffee in hand, Mom searches for a spoon. "Where have all the spoons gone?" When she finds one, she opens the jar of Coffee Mate and looks over at Brian. "Are you dressed?" He has his shirt and pants on. "Good boy, Bri. Now, where are your socks?" Noticing them in his hand, she says, "Go sit on the steps and put on your socks."

As Brian sits on the steps, he struggles to put on his socks. "Bry'n hun'ry…Bry'n want som'thin' to eat…Bry'n hunry," he resumes as he pulls up his sock and starts down the hall to the kitchen, knowing that the kitchen door is locked to keep him from getting in when he's not supposed to.

"After you put on your socks and turn off the TV you can have a piece of toast with peanut butter."

He has already had two pieces of toast with cheese, topped with his morning dose of Depakote, the medicine that helps control his seizures and that is responsible, in part, for his constant hunger. That was an hour ago. It is now almost 6:15 a.m. and he is negotiating for more food. And so the next piece of toast will be but a snack, a snack to ready him for his bus ride, which he eagerly awaits each day.

Sitting at the kitchen table, Brian watches his mother apply the peanut butter to his toast. He pulls back the curtain, "Bry'n bus come soon…" Then he looks back to see if the piece of toast is ready and tries, not too successfully, to hold back from reaching for it.

Noticing, as she does, his every effort, his mom says, "Good, Bri. Your bus will be here in a little while." She hands him the toast, which his mouth meets halfway as his hand takes it from her hand.

Still chewing, and swaying back and forth, Brian holds up his empty cup. "Bry'n thirsty…milk."

"You already had two glasses of milk. You can have water," she responds.

With that he is up and on his way to the sink where he almost fills his plastic cup and, without missing a beat, he is at the freezer. With his ever-trembling hand he removes two, three ice cubes from the plastic box on the door. Making his way back to the table, plopping into his seat, pulling back the curtain to look for the bus, he continues, "What time Arthur on?"

"You know, Brian, Arthur is almost over. He was on at six this morning."

"Sis o'clock," he says, as if on cue sipping the last of his water and looking back out the window. "Naaam yooo ren...," he begins.

"That's it, Bri. Nam myo-ho-renge-kyo...Nam myo-ho-renge-kyo." Mom encourages him to chant for what he wants. As with many things Brian seems to know without really knowing, he knows these words are good for him to say.

Hearing something in the driveway, Mom goes to the door and looks out. Seeing the bus, she turns to come back to Brian, who is already standing in the hall.

"Brian, your bus is here," she says and gathers Brian's stuff.

He is now standing beside her, telling her, just to be sure, "Bry'n bus here." He patiently stands as she finishes buttoning his coat, making sure his lunch money is in his backpack and his hat is on his head. The two go out the door, across the lot. The door to the bus is open and the bus driver greets Brian as he makes his way up the steps and finds his way to a seat near the window.

Mom steps back as the driver closes the door and waves at her smiling Brian.

Watching as the bus backs out, Mom takes a breath of spring and notices the blossoms on the tree in her yard and thinks of all the possibilities that come with spring. She hopes that she will find some for her Brian.

Once back inside the house, she calls from the bottom of the stairs, "Cory...Are you dressed? Come down and eat your breakfast."

Mom returns to her knees and her chanting as her younger son Cory comes down, picks up his toast and returns upstairs to finish watching TV before walking up the street to wait for his bus to take him to his fifth-grade class at the local elementary school.

With her boys gone, Mom chants a little longer before leaving to be the school nurse at an elementary school in the county, hoping that Brian's school won't call. She chants that Brian won't have a seizure. "Nam yo…" and then she is off to her job.

It is 6 p.m. when the threesome walk back into the house and Mom invites her sons to join her in the Buddhist prayer, "Sancho." Cory quickly lips the words and is on his way into the kitchen, then to the solitude of his bedroom.

Taking off his jacket and dropping it near the steps, Brian is on his way to the living room TV when he takes a detour to the kitchen. He asks, "Bry'n have potpie?" and opens the freezer.

"Thank you, Bri. Now go in and watch Arthur while I fix this," says Mom, taking a potpie from her eager helper.

"Bry'n have potpie…Bry'n have potpie…What time Arthur on?" he asks, more out of habit than a need to know.

"He's on now," says Mom, who turns the oven to 350° and goes to the sink to wash her hands. By now Brian is back in the kitchen, opening the drawer next to the stove, pulling out the pot holders and handing them to her.

"Thank you, Bri." She goes on with her tasks, checking the dishwasher.

"Bry'n hun'ry," says Brian as he opens the refrigerator and starts to look inside.

Mom comes over and gently moves him away as she closes the refrigerator door.

"Nothing before supper," she says.

Brian eventually glides into the living room and stands before the TV. He picks up the remote, presses the ON button and then 2 and 6. Mom, who is already kneeling, chanting, half-turns towards her younger son. "Turn it down Bri."

Lowering the volume, Brian stands before the TV and then takes a step onto his small trampoline and begins to bounce.

He bounces with his left hand extended. He moves his wrist and fingers limberly back and forth as he intones an almost whirr-like sound. He is riveted to his TV friend Arthur, the aardvark, and today's adventures until midway through, with his mother still chanting, he quietly makes his way back into the kitchen, opens the refrigerator and finds a blue, plastic-wrapped block of cheddar cheese. As he begins to unwrap it, Mom appears in the doorway, having noticed him missing.

"What are you doing?" she asks, taking the cheese from him and putting it back.

"Nutin'…Bry'n hun'ry."

"What did I say? Nothing before dinner," she reminds him and ushers him out.

He picks up a cup from the dining room table as they pass and he holds it out. "Bry'n thirsty."

"Okay. You can have some water." She escorts him back into the kitchen to be sure he gets only water.

Brian stops at the refrigerator. He opens the freezer door, shakily grabs an ice cube, then a second one from the plastic box and then fills his cup with water at the sink. His mother stands close by. In a minute he is back in front of the TV. This time with his cup of water firmly in his left hand. His left foot taps while his right arm moves back and forth. His mouth is open as he watches Arthur.

When it is nearly time to take the potpies from the oven, Mom goes to the refrigerator and takes a full head of broccoli to the sink. She rinses it, breaks it into manageable pieces. She moves and lifts the lid of the big pot and steps back, away from the steam. As she puts the freshly rinsed pieces of green vegetable onto the small rack that will hold them above the boiling water, she calls to Brian.

"Bri… here help me set the table. She hands him three plates to set on the table but before she can give him the forks and cups and napkins, he is seated on the chair at the window, pulling back the curtain.

"Cory," Mom calls, as she finishes setting the table.

Cory arrives. Brian looks at his younger brother and smiles, "Coor-ee," and returns to looking out the window.

Mom drains the broccoli and puts the three hot potpies on the three plates. She hands Cory one and tells Brian that he will have to wait until his cools. She removes the top crust of Brian's pie as he watches eagerly before turning to finish the dinner preparation.

Brian is again pulling back the curtain and looking out the window. "Joe comin' tonight?' he asks, as he looks out at the parking lot.

"Not tonight Bri," Mom says as she puts three slices of American cheese on the steaming broccoli and puts the lid on top to be sure the cheese melts.

Cory is already peeling back the top crust of his potpie as Brian watches, starts to reach and is rebuffed. "No, Bri. Mom is getting yours," says Cory.

Mom is now at the table and Brian is asking again,"Joe comin' tonight?"

"Not tonight, Bri." Mom says it again, as she brings the two plates with potpies and cheese-covered broccoli to the table. "Cory, don't forget there is broccoli."

One more time Brian wants to know, "Joe comin' tonight? Joe with Jon?" Joe is Mom's boyfriend who is a part of Brian's life. John is Joe's son.

"Yes, Bri. Joe is with John tonight." Mom removes the top of the rather large jar of capsules and places it on the table in front of Brian. Brian fumbles with the bottle as he pours the capsules onto the table. "How many Brian?" she asks.

"For," he tells her.

"Good. Take out four."

Without looking, he puts most back into the bottle.

Mom is ever-patient with her instructions. "Look what you are doing, Bri."

When Brian has four capsules, she sits down with the top crust of the potpie on one plate and the rest on another. Taking one of the two-tone blue capsules, she taps it to be sure most of its contents go to one end. Then, in her well-practiced way, she squeezes and separates the capsule as she sprinkles the contents onto a piece of the potpie crust. Making sure the crust is cool, she folds it and extends it towards Brian's waiting, open mouth. As he takes the bite, he turns and, pulling back the curtain, looks out the window. Turning back, he finishes swallowing, takes a sip of milk and, in a rhythm the two have come to over the years, is back to receive the next piece of medicine-filled crust from his mom who is asking Cory about school.

As Brian finishes his fourth medicine-filled bite, he impulsively reaches for a piece of broccoli from his plate and his mom reminds him to finish chewing what he has in his mouth. Still chewing, he is up, out of his chair.

"Where are you going?"

"Bry'n need ket'sup." He makes his way to the refrigerator.

"For what?"

"Bry'n thirsty."

Mom directs him back to his seat. "You already had your milk and two glasses of water. No more now." At the table, his medicine finished, Mom slides the rest of the potpie in front of him and reminds him to eat one bite at a time.

Focused on his potpie and broccoli, Brian is silent for a moment and then after a couple of reminders to chew and eat only one bite at a time, he is planning tomorrow. "Bry'n have cheese sandwich for br'k f'st. Bry'n go to school tomorrow. No two hour late. Bry'n have pizza for lunch." He almost sings the words as he moves to and fro, flipping the curtain all the while.

His litany continues as Mom clears the table and ushers him out of the kitchen, closes the louvered doors and moves the pieces of hardware to secure the small padlock in place, safeguarding the food from Brian's regular assaults.

Mom segues to the night's next activity. "It's time for your bath, Brian." Upstairs she draws his bath and encourages him to undress and go to the bathroom before he gets into the tub, and she checks to make sure there are enough towels on the floor and that the soap and shampoo are within easy reach.

"La, la, la, la, la," he sings as he steps into the water. He splashes the warm bath water on his legs, which fill the tub. "Bry'n go to school tomorrow?"

"Yes, Bri. You go to school tomorrow," she replies, maneuvering him to his knees so that she can wash his hair. She places shampoo into her hand, bends him over to place his head under the water and begins to lather his head. "Snow days and late days should be over for this year. I know you won't miss them," she tells him.

As she finishes rinsing his hair and helps him sit to finish his bath, he looks at her, almost reaching to turn her face to his, "Cuse me...Cuse me."

"Very good, Bri. Very good to excuse yourself...What is it?"

"Bry'n hun'ry...Pop..pop... pop corn."

She continues washing him. "You want popcorn after all you had today?"

"Yeah," he assures her.

"Okay, after your bath." She rises from the side of the tub. She's always ready for popcorn herself.

"You can play in the water for a little while. Keep the water in the tub."

"Pop-corn. Bry'n have pop-corn later," he reminds her.

"Okay," she says and makes her way out of the bathroom to gather his clothes.

Almost filling the tub, he sits splashing with his hands and singing his own special song that becomes louder and louder. "La, la, la...Nam yo ho..."

A half-step between the bathroom and his room, his mother's voice encourages him. "That's it, Bri. Keep chanting."

"O-O-K."

When she returns, Brian is sitting on the towels on the toilet. She takes a towel and wraps it around his shoulders. "It's time to get dressed." She sets his clothes on the corner of the sink and, after drying him, puts a tee shirt on his head; he pulls his head through, pulling the tee shirt over his arms. Meanwhile, Mom has started his feet into his sweat pants.

"Brian, you are getting so big. I can't believe you're a teenager already. I can remember when you were just a baby crawling around here."

She hesitates and, for an eternal moment, remembers his early childhood—the seizures and the painful realization that something was wrong with her firstborn. Brian was different. The exact reason did not matter, nor would it be determined.

At times, the seizures took over his young life. There were paramedics. There were helicopter rides to Johns Hopkins Pediatric Shock Trauma. There were more than a few visits to emergency rooms, and there was the one time she had to pull off the road because her Brian was seizing so bad.

To Mom, it appeared the doctors didn't believe what she was telling them—how serious her Brian's seizures were—despite the fact that she is an RN. To them, she was just another mother, and you know how excitable, almost hysterical, mothers can be. Then one of their own became a witness. Brian had a grand mal, a seizure of the worst kind, in her doctor's office. That seizure not only caught the doctor's attention, it caused him to call in a colleague, a neurologist who would become Brian's doctor.

Right after that grand mal, or soon after, Brian seemed not to progress. He did not develop intellectually or emotionally as he should. Testing and theories and patterning began. There were meetings with doctors who explored endless possibilities and new approaches. Mom bought equipment and engaged volunteers to help with endless hours of exercising Brian. There were endless sleepless nights. Her vigilance did not, could not cease, only be redefined. In the middle of it all, she found herself alone with Brian and his younger brother. Her husband, unable, had left. She continued her chanting.

Mom wipes away a tear. She and Brian are now making their way downstairs to the kitchen. Brian is almost chanting the words "Bry'n want pop-corn." He sits at the kitchen table and watches as she pours in the olive oil, waits and then drops in a kernel.

"Bry'n want pop-corn."

As soon as the test kernel pops, she pours in enough kernels to cover the bottom of the pot, covers the pot with its lid and gently moves the pot to and fro. Brian listens and smiles as the corn begins to pop. With Mom's hand on the pot handle and her mitted other hand holding down the lid, they listen as the noise increases until, just at the right instant, she turns off the burner, gives the pot a few more shakes and sets it aside.

"Bry'n have popcorn."

"Then off to bed, " she says, pouring the popped corn into plastic containers, then salting each.

"B- E-D…Bry'n want water." He hands her another of his many cups.

"Just a little," she says, half-filling the cup. "You're going to bed and I don't want any accidents."

The two sit at the kitchen table, each with a plastic container of popcorn and a third container for tomorrow. At first he eats a little at a time. Then, as she goes to the refrigerator for something to drink, he begins to shovel the popcorn in by handfuls.

"Brian," she says as she pulls away his less than half-full container, "you can have the rest tomorrow. It is time for bed." She puts the lid on the container.

"What time Bry'n bus come?"

"You know, Bri."

"Sev'n...fif'een," he says, looking at her to hear what she will say, just in case.

"That's right. Now to bed. I want you to sleep all night." She must give him his Risperadal, just to make sure. She sends him to the bathroom, "Go pee and I will bring your medicine and brush your teeth." She brings his favorite cup half-full with a mixture of juice and medicine.

"Bry'n poop," he tells her as he pulls up his pants.

"Drink this."

He does and she asks, "Did you wipe?" She already knows the answer. The pair return to the bathroom. He pulls down his pants. Tearing off some toilet paper she proceeds to clean him as he bends over. She reminds him to flush. She stands at the sink to wash her hands and instructs him to do the same. She leaves to check on the state of his bed. As she returns, he is emerging from the bathroom. "Did you wash your hands with soap and water?"

"Yah." He holds up his hands to show her as he attempts to linger in the hall.

She turns him around, taking him back to the bathroom. She applies toothpaste to his Barney toothbrush as he stands obediently and she completes this one last task for the day. She taps the last drops of water from the toothbrush.

"You are so big, Brian." In fact he nearly fills the small bathroom.

He gives her a hug and kisses her on the forehead. She smiles and they walk into his room. She straightens his bed covers and he gathers his Arthur doll and a take-out menu and his latest set of pictures. "What time Bry'n bus come?" he asks one last time.

"Seven fifteen and now it's time for you to go to sleep," she says, pulling up his covers.

"Bry'n watch TV?" he asks.

"Not tonight." She kisses him goodnight and turns out his light. From the darkened room, Mom hears, "What time Arthur come on?" When she does not answer, he begins, "Nam..."

"That's it Bri…keep chanting."

She returns to the bathroom, turns on the water, lights a few candles and then goes to her room to gather her nightgown and socks. As if on a cruise, she will lie in the warm water and try to relax, thankful for another day without a seizure.

After her bath, she will dress and drag herself down the stairs to kneel before her altar and chant her evening prayers. This is how she began her day and how she will bring it to a close. Finished chanting, she extinguishes the two candles, stands and reverently closes the doors to her Gohonzon. At the foot of the steps she notices Brian sitting at the top.

"Do you want your cheese sandwich for breakfast?" she asks her sleepy-eyed boy.

"Yeeeah…" he replies, yawning.

"Then you better get to bed," she says. Her voice sounds tired but firm.

Reluctantly he goes to his room and his bed. He has one last request. "Cover me up."

"No, I already did that." For that day, if not for that week, Mom is at the end of her nearly endless supply of patience, as if patience comes that way.

She takes the last steps to sit on the edge of her bed. Taking off her robe, she lifts her socked feet from the floor, turns off the light and, as she pulls up the covers, she buries her head into the softness of her pillow. Groping for her bedraggled Grey, what once was some type of stuffed animal, she pulls the day over her head.

It is 4 a.m. when she hears him standing in her room. "Bry'n hun'ry."

The Intruder

THE PAIN WOKE HIM. He did not want to wake. If only he could sleep a few more minutes. No use, he thought. He opened his eyes and looked out the window into the gray, fuzzy morning and then turned to the table at the side of his bed, careful to avoid the brown plastic containers that lined the table. The plastic containers were the troops that were his defense against the pain that had become his only constant companion.

He switched on the lamp. He liked the lamp. It was brushed silver and had a green shade that bore the mark of another of his moves. He lifted his eyeglasses and decided to turn the light off. He'd recently returned to this house where he had lived on the second floor with his second son. It was hard to believe he'd been away for more than ten years. He now lived on the first floor.

He tried not to think about the pain. *If I lie still enough…* He knew better. Thinking of other things and other times did not make the pain go away.

They'd told him there wouldn't be much pain. *Much pain? For whom?* They'd told him about pain with the same authority they'd told him they'd gotten *it* all. That was after the second surgery. He was dying. That he knew. *When,* was anyone's guess.

It was almost dawn. He liked the dawn. He liked watching the dark night turn to gray to a new day. He liked looking out the window at the hodgepodge of homes that was his neighborhood. On good days, when the pain was not too severe or distracting, he would move a second pillow under his head and watch. Through the blinds, which he always kept open, he'd watch as the shapes came into view. It was all a puzzle, the pieces of which were all too familiar. With each passing moment, the pieces took their places to complete the picture of another of his final days.

A noise came from the other room, the kitchen adjacent to his bedroom. Noises in the night had always scared him. Not now. Now he welcomed the sound of something other than his own breathing.

"Hello," he said in a barely audible voice, straining to see or hear anything more. "Hello. Is anyone there?" he asked, propping himself up in the bed.

The second hello brought a shadowy figure into his bedroom. It was too dark to see more. Small in stature, the figure stood at the foot of his bed. The two were silent for a moment before the figure said, "I have a gun. Don't move."

"I wish I could," said the man in the bed. "What do you want? I don't have any money."

"I don't want money," said the figure. "I want to get warm. Do you have any food?"

"Yeah. There's food in the kitchen. Take what you want," said the man in the bed.

The figure stepped back to the doorway and took a look into the kitchen without leaving the room. "What kind of food do you have?" he asked.

"Does it matter?" asked the man.

"Not really," replied the figure.

"I think there is a can of tuna."

"I hate tuna fish. That's all we had to eat at the last place I was."

"And where was that?"

"Why do you want to know?"

"Just curious. If you really just want to get warm, go sit in the kitchen and leave when you're warm."

"Okay."

After a few minutes the intruder again stood in the doorway. "I'm going to leave now."

From the bed came a sleepy, barely audible "Huh."

"You alright?" asked the intruder. When there was no answer, the intruder walked into the bedroom and saw that the man appeared to be sleeping. But he wasn't sure. He stepped closer. With the next step he was at the foot of the man's bed. The intruder's right hand touched the man's blanket, beneath which the man's foot was still.

"Hey! Hey! You all right?"

The man in the bed was very still. The intruder took another step toward the head of the bed and stared at the man's face. The man's eyes were open. The intruder noticed that the blanket over the man's chest was darker than the rest of the blanket.

"Freeze!" came a voice from behind the intruder. "Don't move! Step away from the bed! Put your hands over your head!"

The voice came from a Baltimore City police officer. He was maybe five foot seven and weighed about 185 pounds. Sweat beaded his brow. His brown hands stretched out with a police pistol pointed at the intruder. "Take one step back, slowly."

The intruder complied.

"Now put your hands behind your back," said the officer. In a very practiced motion, the police officer reached, easily removed the handcuffs from his belt and clipped the intruder's hands one to the other. "Sit here!" He directed the man to sit on the floor.

Then, as the officer was on his radio asking for back-up, a second officer, a woman, appeared at the bedroom door, gun drawn.

"Where the fuck you been?" the first officer asked. He couldn't help but notice the drawn Glock. "Put that away..."

"We were on another call," answered the second officer.

The second officer looked to be in her early 20s and seemed nervous. "Oh," said the first officer. "It's you." He recognized the rookie from roll call. "How's your first night going?"

"Fine!" she said. "Whadya got here?"

"Don't know. Had a call from a neighbor that the back door to this place was open. When I got here I found this."

"Hey!" said the intruder. "Is he all right?"

"Is who all right?" the second police officer asked.

"The man."

"What man?"

"The man there in the bed."

It was then that the second police officer looked at the man in the bed. The man's eyes were closed.

The first officer approached, put his index and second finger on the man's throat. "Call 911!" he shouted to the woman officer. Then he saw that the man's bedcover was bloody. He pulled it down, lifted the man's shirt and saw the wound.

From the floor, the intruder shouted, "Can't you see the knife?"

"What knife?" asked the second officer.

"The knife in his hand."

The ambulance came quickly. The paramedics removed the towel the first officer had used in an attempt to stop the man's bleeding. The knife was taken from his hand.

The intruder was taken to the Northeast Precinct where the officer at the desk asked the first officer, "What's this?"

"Not sure. Don't know exactly. Started as what looked like a burglary, but we found a man in a bed with a knife wound."

This was the first hint that the intruder had heard of a connection between the intruder and the man's wound. "What you talking about? I didn't do nothing," he said.

"Yeah," started the desk officer. "That's what everyone says."

"Where do you want me to take him?" asked the first officer.

"How about home?" said the desk officer.

"Funny."

"After you print him, take him to room two."

"What time is it?" asked the first officer.

"Almost seven."

"Shit. I ain't gonna get outta here now."

"Let the rookie take it?" asked the desk officer.

"Not a bad idea."

Just then the second officer walked in.

"Hey Officer Rookie. Here's your first arrest," said the first officer, as he moved the intruder in her direction.

"What?"

"What? Hell. Pay attention," said the desk officer.

"I don't think that is supposed to be how it is done. According to what I learned at the Academy, the first officer on the scene is the arresting officer."

"Well, you are not at the Academy. This won't be too hard. Book him and take him back and get his statement. Ain't nothing gonna happen for awhile. The guy is in the hospital and we'll have to wait to see what happens…"

Nerves

"NERVES," MOM WOULD OBSERVE in her clear and simple way—this aunt or that uncle or cousin had a case of nerves. Cases of nerves were spread through both sides of our family.

To Mom, nerves were when one of the family was not coping well with the world. The world, well, not really *the* world, only their world was getting on their nerves. Their world was most often family. Their spouse, sons, daughters or cousins were shaking them. They were uneasy, uncomfortable. This sometimes happened when someone died. Then, parts of the people surviving died and the people were not sure how to go on living.

To "shake" them out of their shaky situations, some took pills while others had shock therapy. But what usually happened was the person with nerves stopped showing up at family events the same way divorced wives and husbands disappeared.

There was only one psychiatrist I was aware of in McKees Rocks. He had an office on Chartiers Avenue next to a tavern and across the street from a Buick dealership. I never saw him on the street. For that matter, I don't remember seeing anyone go in or come out of the house where he reportedly lived. I knew one person who went to see him.

While Mom never had a case of the nerves, she was nervous. She was always fussing. She was fastidious about how she looked for her husband, Mike, and she always wanted everything to be just right for him, the house and especially the meals because of his ulcers.

Mom had somehow been able to overcome any temptation to give in to the nerves. Her mother had died soon after giving birth to the family's sixteenth child, Sarah, and at age 13, it fell to my mother to raise Sarah and Emily and a couple of the others. The last thing Mom could have afforded would have been a case of the nerves.

So, while I never quite understood what was the real thing about this condition called nerves, I understood that Mom never really had a case of the nerves because, I am quite sure, *she had nerve*: the ability to stand up to anything or anyone who tried to shake her from what she believed in or had to do.

Saturday Night on Broadway

IDA WAS IN CHARGE. She'd finished the dishes before deciding that maybe, if she took Sarah and Emily out of the very warm apartment, if just for awhile, they might settle down and fall asleep early and give her a few moments to sit by herself at the living room window. From there, she could watch and listen to Saturday night on Broadway.

Saturday nights on Broadway, even this Broadway Street, starting at Sandle's Drugstore, the right turn at the second traffic light on Chartiers Avenue, US Route 51, in McKees Rocks, Pennsylvania, even here, Saturday nights were alive—for some.

For some—not many, not most—Saturday night was time to dress up and go out. The work week was over. The house cleaning and car washing was done. Even the few lawns to be cut had been cut. Some would go to the Fireman's Club or the Elks or the Manachor. And some would drive the seven miles to downtown Pittsburgh. Others just got outside—out onto their porches, out onto the street and into the not-so-fresh air: even though it was Saturday, the mills that put the bread on the tables were still spewing smoke and ash.

Ida and the girls lived in a second-floor apartment on Broadway. With two bedrooms and a living room it could sleep more than a few, and it did. There was Pop and his daughters, Ida and Sarah and Emily. Franny and Dorothy had places of their own but were often at the apartment for meals though Pop's eldest, Katherine, had married and had a home of her own. Carl and Asberry and Harry and the other brothers also had married or found their own places. A place had been found for Bobby and Tom: St. Paul's Orphanage.

Ida was not yet fifteen. The last three years had gone by so quickly, they were a blur. Soon after the birth of Sarah, the family's sixteenth child, Ida's days had turned to weeks to months to years of changing diapers, cooking and cleaning and washing clothes. Hers was a life that would have won any monk a spot in heaven. Her mother's death had heralded her adulthood.

Ida never complained. She did what was needed and more. Whether it was walking the floor to quiet infant Sarah or packing a lunch for Pop, she did it. Too often, one of her brothers would stop in with clothes that needed washing and ironing. On one occasion, one brother left his kids with her when his new wife didn't want them in her house. Day in and day out, she took care of her family. She knew no other life and never asked for one, at least not out loud.

So on this one Saturday night that warm July, Ida led the three girls, clad in plain cotton dresses and scuffed brown shoes, down the two flights of stairs. Ida and Emily, the two elder sisters, held Sarah's tiny hands. Ida and Emily counted the steps for a smiling Sarah. "One...two..." At the bottom of the steps, Ida noticed her roller skates sitting in the corner by the door. She hadn't thought they'd made the move.

Outside, it was almost dark and the lights from the stores were on. A steady stream of people sauntered down the sidewalk and shiny cars passed up and down the street. You could hear the echo of music from the juke box at the Forest Inn, which was only a few doors away. Later in the evening, that music would be drowned out by raucous laughter and other boisterous behaviors of the Saturday night fun seekers. Broadway was busy.

The three girls sat in their doorway, looking out. Ida sat between Emily and Sarah, who clung to their Ida as if she was their mother. Ida listened to the echoing juke box, watched as the women in their summer cotton dresses and high-heeled shoes walked alongside their husbands or boyfriends in their baggy pants and handsome hats. She inhaled the evening, the elixir of ladies' cologne and men's aftershave. Watching the couples, Ida said, so her two younger sisters might think she was talking with them, "I wonder where they're going? Maybe down the Rocks to a dance?"

Ida took it all in and smiled to be outdoors watching Broadway on a Saturday night. But even as the younger girls, unsure, held onto her, she began to think to herself, *If only I could skate down the block, turn around and come back, I would never lose sight of them. I'm sure they would sit still and watch me. They would.*

Making sure Emily kept hold of Sarah's hand, Ida fetched her skates. Then sitting back down between the girls, she spun the metal skate wheels to be sure they would still spin and fastened them to her shoes using the skate key to tighten one then the other.

"Ya wanna see Ida skate?" she asked. The question filled her with an excitement she hoped they would pick-up on. "Ida's gonna skate down to the corner and come back. Yinze are going to sit here and watch Ida go down to the corner and come back. Wouldn't you like to do that?"

"Yeah!" Emily said, nodding her head. Sarah nodded her head in agreement too.

Ida moved Sarah closer to Emily, making sure Emily held Sarah's hand. "Now, Emily, you are gonna sit here and keep Sarah company. Sarah, now you sit here with Emily and watch Ida skate down the street and skate back to you and Emily. Okay?" She looked close into Sarah's brown eyes. "Okay. Now you watch. You watch Ida…"

With the skates fixed to her shoes, Ida stood. She lifted and shook her right foot and then her left to make sure the skates were on tight. Rolling in front of the two expectant faces, she said, "It's been so long. I hope I don't fall."

She skated a few feet testing her balance. Then, with her head turning back and forth between the two girls and the sidewalk, she started to skate. One foot in front of the other she rolled down the sidewalk. She felt the rhythm coming back to her. She felt the strength of her legs pushing her as she gained speed. Emily clapped and Sarah clapped as their Ida made her way away from them.

The Saturday night breeze cooled Ida's face as she pushed her way between the walkers. And, before she knew it, she was almost to the corner. As she looked back to be sure her charges were still where she had left them, she thought, just for an instant, about not turning back. She thought about going on, around the corner and around the block. But those thoughts quickly dissipated at the thought of the girls.

Two voices called, "Ida! Ida!"

She slowed to her sisters' reaching arms. "Emily and Sarah see Ida skate?" she asked.

"Ida…" Emily began, "Ida went all the way down to the end."

"Now," began Ida, pulling each sister close, "you knew I would come back."

"Ida go away…" Sarah started to cry.

Holding her Sarah to reassure her, as their mother would have done, Ida took another breath of Saturday night. "You know I wouldn't leave you. Do you want me to carry you up the steps and put you and Emily to bed?"

Ida smiled, pleased with herself as she looked to the street. She now felt a part of the group that moved along Broadway. Removing her skates and placing them behind the door where she had found them, she turned to lead the way up the stairs. She wondered if there was a treat she could give before she put the girls to bed. *I can still skate,* she thought, though she knew she had more important things to do.

Peeping Tom

THE BOYS WERE BATHED and in their pajamas. It was spring and some of the screened windows were open. The lamp between their twin beds lit the room like a Rockwell painting. As the boys knelt to say their prayers, their mother stood over them to be sure they got the words right.

Then, from the alleyway, they heard their father's voice. "Don't move! Step away from the window and put up your hands. I have a gun."

"Don't move," the mother echoed as she covered the boys in their beds. "I'll be right back."

From their beds the two boys could hear the back door open and the mother and father's muffled voices. Then they heard their father say, "Ida, call the police!" Then, from the kitchen, he asked, "Are the boys okay?"

"They're in bed," she said.

"Go in with them, so I can take *him* into the living room."

The boys' bedroom served as a passageway to the rest of the apartment. The mother entered the bedroom first and stood between the twin beds. The father pointed the .22 automatic pistol he'd brought home from the shooting range at the teenager's back. They walked by the boys in their beds.

"Sit down over there," said the father from the living room, as the mother dialed for help.

"Hello! This is Ida Chamberlin. I live at 760 Mary Street. Yes. I'm Mike's wife. He caught someone peeping into our window. Could you send someone up here?"

Before long, the police arrived. By then the two young boys had summoned enough courage to crawl out of their beds to the vantage point of their parents' bed in the next room. From there they could not only hear but see most of what was going on.

One of the police officers pulled out a small lid lined with brown wax paper taken from the teenager's pocket. Right in the lid's center was a hole, a hole not much bigger than a pin, yet big enough to allow a person to see into windows.

"This," the police officer started to explain and the father finished, "is one of the tools of the trade of a peeping Tom."

Anticipation

PITTSBURGH IN FEBRUARY WAS as cold as it was dark. Sunset was at five o'clock in the afternoon; yet, by four o'clock, streetlights were on to pierce the darkness hastened by the soot and ash from the steel mills. We looked forward to the little bit of brightness that came with snow, even though its white covering did not last long. Soon the soot from the mills made the snow a dark gray.

As I recall those long, dark days of what seemed to be never-ending winter in the late 1950s, I remember the importance of looking forward to something to look forward to.

My memory has it as a Monday. We were through and past Sunday afternoon and the dread of another school week. And Tuesdays there would have been basketball games: The noise of the games and the pleasure of sneaking a few cigarettes in the boys' bathroom while we talked about all we would do when the weather changed, which would make us think it worth the wait.

So, on a Monday I was trudging my way along the frozen alley behind Mary Street just about where it joins Margaret Street. Almost to the corner where I would round to get to Grindy's grocery (to buy a half-pound of summer bologna so Mom could fry it for our lunch-time sandwiches), I stopped. I wasn't really thinking of anything, except everything that *might be,* someday. I paused and tilted my face to feel the sun. Closing my eyes, I could almost hear the splashes and laughter, months away, from the nearby pool.

At my feet I noticed a crevice in the snow. I watched a thin stream of water, which had been ice since the November freeze. It was clear and clean. I could even hear it moving as I stopped to follow its path through the snow to Margaret Street. And as I watched the water melt the snow, it uncovered the alley beneath— and a Popsicle stick partially stuck in the snow.

Reaching down, I freed the sign of summer gone and moved it out into the stream, and I watched it float to the end of the alley in search of spring.

Ice Sliding

THE BLACK MACADAME SCHOOLYARD was covered with ice and snow. It was almost seven o'clock on a weekday evening and I was on my way home when I noticed the glaze. I surveyed the scene, coming to the place I thought I would begin. The idea was to run along the snow and ice until I thought it was time—*then I would slide*. My first attempts were met with resistance. There was too much snow. I could only slide a short distance. But I kept at it.

With each run I increased the length of my slide. Eventually, I slid from five to ten, well, probably three to five feet. But I kept making it longer.

I was completely alone there in the yard, which most of the time was filled with voices of children. I liked the quiet. I liked the moon lighting my way. So, I kept sliding and was very pleased with myself. There, alone, I sang my own praises of how good I was at this winter's night sport. *I am sliding like a champion.*

Then I decided I would slide down to the basketball pole, grab on and swing around. Yes. I would slide and grab and turn around. The first time it worked. Now I am sliding like a champion and adding the twist. *Oh, am I good! Where is everyone?*

Getting enough speed was important. Standing almost at the back wall of the yard, I prepared myself to run. I began. Then I ran a little faster. I was really moving. Then I hit the ice. I was gliding so smoothly. The pole was right there. I reached out my arm to grab on to it so that I could do the twist.

BAM! I am not sure what happened, but my face hit the pole. The pole's cold metal shocked me. I found myself on the ground. Had the moon blinded my eyes? Was I tired? I slipped. My hand still on the pole, I pulled myself to it. I was still on the ground.

My glasses. Did I break my glasses? I laid there a minute trying to figure out what had happened. My glasses seemed to be all in one piece. I stood and brushed off the very cold ice. My face hurt. It was time to go home.

Slowly I walked across the schoolyard. Under the street light at the corner of Mary and Margaret streets in front of the Reynolds house, I tried to survey what I might have done to my coat and pants—nothing too apparent. My left leg hurt. My face hurt even more. I continued up Mary Street to our house.

Inside the door, there on the landing that connected the two sets of steps, one into the basement, the other up into the kitchen, I took off my coat. By now Mom was at the kitchen door, "Is that you, Joe?"

"Yeah," I said, trying to reassure her and me that it was me and that I was alright.

From the kitchen, Mom wanted to know where I had been. Fortunately, my face was red from the cold so she did not notice what I would discover when I got to the bathroom after I'd excused myself.

My glasses were bent and only one side of my reddened face seemed to be getting less red. The other side was not only red, it was swollen. I stood there looking into the bathroom mirror, hoping to make it go down. It only got worse. Now what was I going to do? The glasses were bent at the temple. I could only hope that, after awhile I might be able to bend them back, close to what they were supposed to be.

It was one of those nights I might have to go to bed early. Dad and my brother Mick were out, so there was a chance that, if Mom was watching TV, the living room would be dark and her "bad eyes," as she referred to them, would allow me to slip in and catch a couple shows without notice.

We silently watched TV and, as the evening wore on, I became more aware of the pain in my leg and my eye. At ten o'clock I decided to go to bed.

It was the next morning when Mom noticed my black eye. "What happened to you?" she asked.

"What?" I asked.

"Your eye is swollen. Were you in a fight?"

"Oh! That...I fell on the ice on the way home last night."

She left me for a minute to go to the bottom of the steps where she called upstairs. "Mickey! Are you up?" she asked. She set my grapefruit in front of me and called again, "Mickey! You are going to be late for school!" Then, again looking at my eye, she said, "Are you sure you are alright?"

I ate my grapefruit and drank my milk-filled coffee and was on my way out the door as Mick made his way down the stairs.

"Hey! Aren't you going to wait for me?" he asked.

"And be late? " I asked, turning to him.

"Whoa! What happened?"

"Whadya mean?"

"Your eye. It's swollen. Who'd you tangle with? And your glasses are bent."

"Slipped on the ice on my way home last night."

I was out the door and down the street, past the seven houses, and to the schoolyard. I stopped at the Reynold's house, took the three steps to cross the street and stood there for a moment. My sliding place was now covered with the feet of grade school kids waiting for the bell to call them inside from the cold. I walked across the schoolyard and slipped through the fence to get to Mrs. Hess's where Timmy and Terry were enjoying a pre-school cigarette.

Timmy noticed first. "What happened?"

"You won't believe it," I began, as I told the tale of my near-perfect slide and then my almost-fatal accident on the night ice there in the schoolyard.

"Got a smoke? " I asked.

The Laslos

I CAN STILL HEAR the sound of Timmy's body sliding inside the blue cloth-covered wooden casket as we pallbearers started up the second set of salt-covered concrete steps.

Chartiers Avenue, in front of St. Francis de Sales Church, was impassable that last Friday in January 1960. It was not the snow. It was the two hearses lined up behind three other hearses.

The church was full. It did not seem real. It could not be that they weren't coming back. No more of Terry's grins or Tommy's sullen ways or Timmy's angry finger in your face. No more watching Sam Laslo fetch his wife's beer as she sat smoking her unfiltered cigarettes, explaining the world to us as we waited for Timmy and Terry.

In their tiny, low-ceiling kitchen, with its darkened doorway to the dirt floor coal cellar, she had sat making sure her boys understood the rules. Lucy's rules. Lucy's rules allowed her boys to stay out late, wear real leather motorcycle jackets and boots and smoke. Timmy had once gone face to face with the one-armed manager of the Roxianne movie theater when told to put out his cigarette because he was not old enough to smoke. "I'm allowed to smoke!" said Timmy, taking one more drag before stepping it out. One of Lucy's rules was to be respectful to adults.

The Laslos were different. They were just a little tougher than most of the people who lived in the Rox, and a little poorer. Their small kitchen was in a red insulbrick house tucked back between two other houses. At first glance, you might have mistaken it for a garage. But that very weekend they had moved into their new, second-floor apartment above one of the stores across from

St. Francis de Sales church on Chartiers Avenue. I had forgotten all about the move.

THE LAST TIME I'd seen them I was with my brother, Mick, at confession on Saturday night. And a good thing, because the night before at the basketball game at Canevin High School, we were outside smoking and Timmy—*or was it Terry?*—had one of those magazines, you know, with the naked ladies. Shiny women with large, round breasts, inviting impure thoughts. I don't remember if I confessed to having looked at the images I was still trying to imagine. Not sure of the exact nature of such a sin, I only knew there was something worthy of looking forward to.

Leaving confession, we said a goodnight that became a goodbye. As they walked down the hill to their new apartment, and we up to our house on Mary Street, we said we'd see them in church at the nine o'clock Mass the next morning. If we missed seeing them at church the next morning, I don't remember. Lucy's rules sometimes allowed for missing Mass.

Monday I'd gotten home from school early enough to go to the gym and the intramural basketball coach asked me to take Terry's jersey. He hadn't shown-up for practice, again.

As I left the gym, I walked to the alley at the top of the schoolyard, halfway up Margaret Street. That is where the dream began. Paul Gill stopped me and asked, "Did you hear?"

"Hear what?"

"About the Laslos? They're dead!"

"Can't be!" I said, clutching Terry's jersey. "I just saw them Saturday night."

"It was on the radio," Paul said. "A McKees Rocks family was found dead in their apartment on Chartiers Avenue."

"No!" I said. "They live on Frank Street."

Hurrying away, I started down Margaret Street and noticed a crowd at the bottom of the hill where Margaret Street intersects with Chartiers Avenue. There at the foot of the hill across from the

De Sales steps was a crowd of people and ambulances and police cars and lights. Lots of lights. I got as close as the side steps to the church. Standing there, struggling to comprehend, I noticed one of our priests coming across the street.

As the cleric approached, he looked at me and, reaching out, touched my arm and answered my unasked question. "It's true. They are all gone," he said as he walked past me to the rectory.

Someone nearby was holding a radio. *A family of five was found dead in their McKees Rocks apartment today. They had just moved into the apartment over the weekend. Sam and Lucy and their three sons: Tommy, age 15, Timmy, age 13, and Terry, age 11, were found. They were apparently victims of carbon monoxide. The preliminary investigation points to a faulty space heater.*

Tommy, the oldest son, reportedly had come home late and found the others unconscious. He attempted to drag his father out, but the fumes were too much. He passed out and was found slumped over his father, who had already died.

I ran home.

Unable to hold back the tears, I was barely able to open the door to the cellarway and stopped on the landing. Hearing me, my mother opened the door to our apartment at the top of the stairs. "They're dead! They're all dead!" I cried.

"Who's dead?" she asked, helping me up the stairs to our kitchen and into a chair.

"The Laslos all died in some kind of accident." I think part of me thought that saying the words would help me wake-up.

The next morning on the bus to school, I sat quiet, somberly thinking about the Laslos, especially Timmy and the times we had fought. We'd fought regularly when we were younger. And the only thing worse than the fight was the balling out my father gave Mick and me—especially my brother—not so much for me losing the fight, as for him not helping me out, as Terry did Timmy. Another of Lucy's rules. Her boys stuck together.

The bus was warm and there was a certain comfort, a distraction in going all the way to the base of the Hill District where I had begun my studies to become a priest at the Bishop Wright Latin School. Then someone opened the newspaper and there on the front page, on the very quiet, nearly full bus, were their five pictures. It took all I had to hold back the tears.

At school, Father Knorr expressed his sympathy, offered a prayer and assured me that it would be all right for me to miss school to attend the funeral.

McDERMOTT'S FUNERAL HOME was packed on Thursday. Not since one of the high school kids had been accidentally shot and killed in a classmate's basement had there been so many kids from the school. Most of us had been there to see Jake the Milkman and the Choo-Choo Man, characters from our lives, who had died, so that we might learn about dying and viewings and funerals. Now, two of the largest rooms were lined with the five Laslo caskets: Sam, Lucy, Tommy and Timmy and Terry.

As one of the pallbearers, I watched as a funeral director gently lifted the pillows from beneath each of their heads before lowering the casket lids. They instructed us where to stand and when to lift the coffin in and out of the hearse and onto the silver cradle with its straps that would lower them into their new home.

It snowed all morning and still the cars lined the road to the cemetery. As the crowd gathered, we all listened and watched as the priest sprinkled the black ashes on the white snow each casket had collected. The priest said a final prayer and closed his book. As we quietly walked back up the hill, the cold wet cemetery began to seep through my shoes.

Smiley

IT WAS A GRAY February Sunday morning in 1968 when I walked up the hill with her after nine o'clock Mass. We made our way slowly up Margaret Street alongside De Sales church and school, built in the early 1900s and named for a Dominican priest, St. Francis de Sales. It was the neighborhood school we'd all attended and it was the church where, less than a year earlier, she'd married her Bobby, whom we called Smiley.

Very lonely—half angry, half sad—she described his letters as we came to the edge of the silent schoolyard. Her steps, slow and deliberate, punctuated her sentences. "He's there and says he likes it...Lots of action. Whatever *action* is..." Her words dripped with sarcasm. Her eyes stared straight ahead as if she was looking for someone.

As we parted, I to my mother's house, she to hers on Railroad Street, two hills higher, I saw her smile when I said, "See ya, Mrs. Rosenwald."

Not more than two weeks later, I was home again. I was home a lot. It was my senior year at The College of Steubenville and the trip, which had seemed very much longer just three years before, was little more than an hour's drive. I was home for a job interview with the Pittsburgh City Schools. And to be with my fiancée, Judy. We would be married in June of that barely new year. And, while Smiley would not be in our wedding, as I was in his, Evelyn would be there.

It was my father who told me. He always seemed to be telling me things I did not want to hear. "Your friend," he said, fighting back tears, struggling for words, "Your friend Rosenwald. He was, was…killed."

Dad didn't have to say where. I knew he was in Vietnam. He did say something about some battle. Then he handed me the *Pittsburgh Post-Gazette*: *Pfc. Robert John Rosenwald of McKees Rocks who had been in Vietnam since early January, has been killed in action there, the Defense Department announced…Pfc. Rosenwald died from wounds he received last Thursday when he was hit by small arms fire while on a combat operation.*

What are small arms I asked myself, and what must it be like to be shot and to lie there wondering if you were going to die? And who was with him on that Thursday? Did he have a chance to smoke one more Lucky?

The next day, as I sat waiting for my job interview with the public schools, I thought about all of us. We were just beginning to take our place, find our way, and now Smiley was gone.

SMILEY WAS ONE of four GI's from Western Pennsylvania on the list that day. He wasn't the first to die from McKees Rocks. He would not be the last. But, he was the closest to me even though one of the others, Bobby Kotik, had been a neighbor from across the street. For Dad, Kotik was probably the closest. Kotik had been drafted into the Marines and I remember how incredulous he'd been. "The Marines!" he'd said the day he left. Dad had been in the Marines at Iwo Jima. When Kotik went into the Corps, they had a connection.

We'd learned of Kotik's death the summer before that February we were becoming stuck in. When you live on a street as small as Mary Street for as long as we lived there, you not only know everyone's cars, you know when they come and go. It was mid-day and everyone was where they were supposed to be—at work or like Dad, waiting to go to work on the second shift, 4 p.m. to 12 a.m. Dad was trimming or cutting something that no longer grows out front when a strange car caught his eye. The car was one thing. But when it parked on our side of the street and the Marines got out, Dad sat down on the step where he'd been standing, sat down in the middle of the day and buried his face in his hands. He knew why they were on Mary Street. There was only one reason. His boy, or the boy across the street. Both were in the U.S. Marine Corps. While Kotik was already there, his son Mick was in the Caribbean training to go to Vietnam.

Maybe it was a mistake.

When Dad opened his eyes, he saw them walking, almost marching to the house across the street and all he could do was cry. Cry in relief and cry for the family and their boy, Lance Corporal Robert Kotik.

Kotik's casket was closed, supporting his mother's belief that he was not really dead.

WE CALLED HIM Smiley because he seldom did. Not until her. It had been a raw February night when she'd come into Ted's Dairy on Chartiers Avenue as if on a mission. We were sitting, talking, drinking coffee and smoking cigarettes, and listening to each other—just in case one of us actually said something. It was our nightly ritual. Then she danced in and asked, "What younse doing?"

"What's it look like we're doing?" Smiley had said, half-turning to look to see who she was looking at. "We're drinking coffee, trying to get warm. It's cold out there. Frigid."

As if on cue, she moved closer. Reaching out, offering her hand, she whispered with a seductive smile, "I'm not frigid. I'll warm you up."

In a moment, if it took that long, he was up from his stool and they were on their way to the door and out into the dark February night. One of us—probably every one of us sitting there—was probably thinking *At least someone might get warm tonight.*

The next day, in Sister Timothy's Algebra II class, I watched as he covered the brown paper book cover he'd scribbled with her name: EVELYN.

Smiley was very good with numbers. In Sr. Timothy's Algebra II class where I sat in the back for a study hall, he was matching wits with the other four members of the class. This was his time. With Xs and funny symbols, he was equal to and, more often than not, ahead of the others. Here he had something to say, while in most of his classes, he was silent.

One of six children, Smiley was the youngest of two girls and four boys, and he received the special attention that came with that place in the family. He always had a pack of cigarettes tucked under the sleeve of his white tee shirt, money in his pockets and gas in his white Ford.

Now that there was Evelyn, he was in line for the phone at Sandle's. He had someone to talk with and wait for, someone to look forward to be with when he was not in school or with the guys at Sandle's counter or across the street on the gray steps of Jowe's Refrigeration at the corner of Chartiers Avenue and Broadway.

I WENT TO his viewing Saturday night at the McDermott Brothers Funeral Home, less than a mile from Sandle's Drugstore, up Chartiers Avenue. On a black felt board below the white plastic letters, Pfc. Rosenwald, a white arrow pointed down the hall. Slowly, I walked into Smiley's room where Evelyn sat inconsolably rocking to the sound of her own teary voice, asking questions that no one answered.

I reluctantly approached. At first she did not recognize me. When she did, she cried out, "Joe! What am I going to do?" Shaking and wanting an answer I did not have, she allowed me to sit with her as I searched for words that did not come.

Just twenty-one years old myself, I was not sure what to do or say to console the widow of one of my best boyhood friends. This was the first time, but would not be the last, I saw tears that were tears of rage as much as tears of sorrow, abandonment.

Two days later, we stood on a crisp February Monday morning listening to the unsung words of "Day is Done"— done much too soon—and watched as the soldiers, reverently, almost routinely, folded the American flag, which they presented to Evelyn "on behalf of a grateful nation." As she pulled it close, hoping it might give her more warmth than her black wool coat, it caught her tears.

We were silent and still, watching as the young girl we knew became the widow we would come to know, and I asked myself, "Why?"

The Death Rattle

OUR DAD LAY IN the middle of the ICU while people moved about tending to him and the others in the room. The room was cold. His arms were connected by tubes to machines that pumped fluid into his body and breath into the plastic mask that covered his face. He was 59 years old.

"I heard the death rattle," Mom whispered. She would repeat it more than a few times.

It was a gurgle. I thought it came from his oxygen mask. But Mom was certain. It was the sound of death those who have been with the dying recognize. And death was not a stranger to her. She'd buried brothers and sisters. When she'd been just 12 years old, she'd buried her mother.

"I heard it," she said. "It was the same sound I heard when…" I don't remember who she remembered, but the sound had pierced her and brought death into the room.

Mom leaned close to let Dad know she was there. My brother Mick and I told him we loved him.

Death, I thought, might be near but I was not as certain as she was. I looked at his face, asleep, as I'd so many times seen it as he lay on the couch napping. He sometimes snored. I'd never heard him gurgle but I had imagined what he would look like if he died. Now I was looking at him as my mother foretold his death.

The nurses said they would be moving him soon. "We'll call if there is a change."

EARLIER, ON MONDAY of that week, Dad had called. "They found a spot on my lung. They are going to operate on Friday."

I'd told him I loved him, remembering the difficult times in our relationship, and finished the fish I was cleaning on our porch in Havre de Grace, Maryland.

ON FRIDAY MORNING, arriving at Mercy Hospital there on the "Bluff" high above the Allegheny River in Pittsburgh, I went to Dad's room, 558, and looked in. The mattress was folded in half.

About one o'clock that afternoon a nurse came to the waiting room to tell Mom and Mick and me that Dad would be going into the operating room soon. When the doctor finally emerged from the O.R., it was about four o'clock. He was wearing a suit and smoking a cigarette. "We think we got it all," he said.

It was about four o'clock the next morning when the hospital called, asking me to come right away. When I got there, Mom and Mick were already sitting in a barely lit room across from a man in a white coat. The scene was Hopperesque.

"He's gone," Mom said.

The doctor asked if we wanted to see him.

Mom waited while Mick and I went to his room. His mouth was open. His eyes were closed. The sheet was neatly pulled up under his chin.

"It's not him," I said to Mick, who quickly stepped out of the room.

When we got back to the house Mom was on the couch crying, "What am I going to do?"

THAT SATURDAY AFTERNOON, we took Dad's favorite suit, white shirt and tie, and his cameo and Knights of Columbus rings and Marine tie tack to McDermott's funeral home. There were lots of decisions. The only one I remember is the cherry wood casket.

The three of us arrived back at McDermotts's that evening. The funeral director instructed us to go in alone for a few minutes before the rest of the family.

From the side of Dad's coffin, Mom reached in, placed her hands on his shoulders and, as if in slow motion, lifted his now dead body. "What did you to do to me?" she screamed.

The funeral director motioned me away. "Let her go."

TUESDAY MORNING ,WE took him to church for Mass and kind words from one of his longtime priest friends. I could not contain the tears that came with the memories.

The drive to Resurrection Cemetery was too quick. Afterwards, Mick took Dad's flag to the house while the rest of us gathered at Aunt Jean's, the house where Dad had been born. I sat and listened as the family told stories about our dad. It was as if I was being wrapped in a family quilt.

A North Avenue Odyssey

IT WAS A SHINY black bug—you know, a Volkswagen Beetle complete with a winding sun roof for air conditioning and the ever-reliable engine warming system for the winter months. I had parked it on North Avenue outside the building where we were teaching for the Harbor City Learning Center, an alternative high school for dropouts: students *and teachers*. We had space in an African American business building. The door between the business men and us was always kept locked.

I came outside. My car was gone. Had I parked it in another place, perhaps Eutaw Street around the corner? More likely, one of my students had borrowed—no, stolen it.

I decided to walk down to Jonah House to call the police. Jonah House was where Phil Berrigan, his wife Liz McAllister, their children and some other members of their resistance community lived. For them, resistance meant periodic time in jail. After spending a day in jail on the last day of the White House Prayer-ins, I had decided to pursue other venues to change the world. Still, I knew I could go there to make a phone call.

This would not be a long walk; but some might have questioned the wisdom of walking from North Avenue to Park Avenue. As one of my students had pointed out, those who are up to less-than-legal things often can read a potential victim's fear and trembling.

Walking to Park Avenue I remembered my first visit to North Avenue. It was to see the play, *The Trial of the Catonsville Nine*. It was the story of Phil and his brother Dan, both priests, and seven others who in May 1968 removed draft cards from the Draft Board in Catonsville, took the cards out to the parking lot, poured on a mixture of their own blood and homemade napalm, and set the cards on fire, calling them "death certificates," as they then waited for the police.

The play had been at Center Stage, on North, less than a mile from Park, on the other side of Charles. Charles Street is *the* street in Baltimore, Maryland. It divides the city into east and west. It connects south to north—the Federal Hill area and Inner Harbor and any number of businesses and restaurants and goes north all the way to the county and the beltway. When people speak of North Avenue they often ponder its dangers, never stopping to think of the less obvious dangers that lie at either end of Charles.

Just down from North Avenue, still on Charles, is the Charles Theater, the best place to see "films" in Baltimore. Next door is Sophie's Crepes, which is adjacent to the Everyman Theater. Across the street is Club Charles, where one might see John Waters, one of Baltimore's premier celebrities.

Further east on North, where I used to shop at Sears is now the Eastern District Court house. It was there I was summoned to answer charges that I had been stalking my ex-wife. The only problem was that I was at Deep Creek Lake on the other side of the state.

Perhaps my most pleasant stop on North Avenue was Leon's Pig Pen. There were two: one at the corner of Greenmount and North, the other near Charles Street. Leon's was often a Friday night destination. The first Friday of each month the Bolton Hill Memorial Episcopal Church hosted a one-hour happy hour, replete with martinis, whiskey sours, wine and homemade appetizers. Afterward, we often gathered at someone's Bolton Hill home, with a couple of us more adventurous ones going to Leon's to fetch ribs and collard greens.

Another favorite North Avenue memory is O'Dell's. It was the disco destination and touted itself as a place where "You'll know if you belong."—I never went.

I turned the corner and started up Park Avenue. There was the car. It was unlocked. I had the key. Since I had not yet called the police, I decided to steal it back.

The Haircut

CHANGE. I USED TO think I was a champion of change. At work, I was at the center of more than a few efforts that focused on change. *Bring it on!*

Then I was sitting in the barber shop, except now I think I am supposed to call it a styling salon, as my younger son gave directions to the barber. (I really think that with a name like Sal, you can still refer to him as a barber.) I watched as my child, my now young man, clearly explained how he wanted his hair cut.

Just a minute before I'd been ready to go out to the car and get something to do, some work, and then, like other times in my busy life, I noticed that something had happened: My little boy was not a little boy anymore. He was a young man. He had grown older and somehow I hadn't noticed, or hadn't wanted to notice.

Where had the time gone?: "Is this the little girl I carried? Is this the little boy at play?," sings Tevya in *Fiddler on the Roof.*

For whatever reason, my son had changed right before my eyes—my eyes that had been too busy looking in other directions. Wow! Look, I thought. He is telling the barber how he wants his hair cut. And all he needs from me is the money.

This was a different kind of moment with my son. I'd been there for it. I'd been open to it. I'd recognized it. Having taken the time to stop and experience it, I was all the richer for it. A memory had been born in the newness of that moment of change: the passage of my little boy to a young man with a fresh haircut.

The Drink

FOR SOME UNKNOWN REASON, Dad had decided to stop at the Commonwealth with my little brother and me. The Commonwealth was one of the bars that punctuated our walk down Chartiers Avenue. For me, this would be an adventure that would not turn out as hoped. Instead, it would become one of those anticipated moments that turns from excitement to uncertainty that borders on fear.

Dad and Mom and my brother and I had walked past this place many times, and I'd always been curious as to what went on in there. Music and laughter often spilled from the occasionally opened door. There were always people. Many were laughing and having a good time, especially on Friday and Saturday nights. More than once, someone had stumbled out, glassy-eyed, wreaking of smoke and alcohol. But this was a week day afternoon.

Dad sat us up on the stools and ordered us ginger ales and himself a shot of something. He sat there smoking his Pall Mall and staring at the shot. Though it was summer, mid-day, and the door was open, the sun did not brighten the barroom. It was dark, made darker by the line of sullen men, elbows holding them up along the long trough-like bar, as if the bar was some type of altar. Most of the men were alone or with one other person whom they occasionally spoke to, seemingly more to lecture than to engage in conversation. "Let me tell you…"

Otherwise, words were few, replaced by sign language that told the bartender when to pour another shot or when to bring another beer or both. Across from the bartender were several shelves of bottles. The bartender moved up and down his runway, reached for the right bottle to pour and which empty glass to fill when a patron placed it on the bar. He seemed to know most of the people, each man seemingly in his own world, sitting near the others only for the purpose of drink.

Most of the patrons stared, stared into their drinks or into the smoke of their cigarettes. Some talked to themselves. Dad simply sat there. He stared at his shot for the longest time, looking at it as if it was looking at him, maybe talking to him. And while others sat there having one shot, then another, with many shots followed by slugs or sips of beer, Dad did not have a beer, only the shot before him. He did not touch it—not to bring it close, not to push it away.

While no one seemed to care that our dad wasn't drinking, one or two did note that there was a shot not being drunk. My brother and I were more interested in the music coming from the juke box across the room.

We had never seen Dad drink anything but coffee, which he drank by the gallon. On occasion, when his ulcer was acting-up, he drank buttermilk. Coffee and Pall Malls were the mainstays of his diet. He did not have one without the other. Most of the time when he drank his coffee he talked to whomever was close. Mostly, that was my mother, even if he was in the dining room and she was in the kitchen.

That day in the bar there was no conversation. Finishing his Pall Mall, he crushed it into one of the numerous ashtrays that lined the bar. "Let's go," were his only words.

As Dad stood to help us off our stools, I noticed that the shot was still there. My brother and I said nothing.

We walked back, up Chartiers onto Island Avenue and up Mary Street hill to our first-floor apartment. Dad stopped in the kitchen to sit at the table and have a cup of coffee with Mom. My brother and I asked to go outside to play.

We never spoke of that day or our visit to the bar or the abandoned shot. The next time we were in a bar with Dad, it was a place on the Northside, referred to as the "chapel" because of its well-behaved patrons. The four of us went there to eat fish sandwiches. Dad drank his more-than two cups of coffee while Mom and Mickey and I drank ginger ale.

Dad's Gift

SEVEN MILES WEST AND north of where the Allegheny River joins the Monongahela sits McKees Rocks, Pennsylvania, the first stop on the Ohio River. And there, off Margaret Street, past St. Frances de Sales Church, is 760 Mary Street, my second stop in life but nonetheless a place of important firsts.

There in that house is where my life began, almost two years after I was born. There is where I learned of family and love. There, I celebrated my first Christmas, my first memory.

I was adopted, you see, as a toddler. The man and woman who would become my parents, Mike and Ida Chamberlin, lived on the first floor of 760, renting from John and Sophie Marmak, who lived upstairs. When my parents considered adopting children, they asked Sophie's opinion. And without hesitation she said yes. Then, as the process began, they learned I had a brother.

"Don't even think of separating those brothers," Sophie told them. "You will adopt them both."

So began my life, and my brother Mickey's, on Mary Street over 60 years ago. Our apartment was cozy. Mom and Dad's bedroom, situated off the living room, was the only way into the room Mickey and I shared, which sat next to the kitchen. Between the living room and my parents' bedroom were sliding doors. Stained to look like oak, they remained open throughout the year—except for the weeks between Thanksgiving and Christmas.

We were still eating leftover turkey sandwiches on toast with mayonnaise, and skillet-warmed stuffing, when my father pulled them closed—right after he moved the Motorola and one of the living room chairs around the corner into the bedroom. It made

73

for a very snug corner where my brother and I would watch TV, one of us in the chair or on the floor, the other sometimes stretching out on the bed as Dad made endless trips behind the doors.

After moving the saw horses and large pieces of platform plywood into the living room, he brought in the boxes. Mickey and I were instructed to look away. And mostly, resisting temptation, we did.

Dad usually worked on this project in the morning. Because he was on the second shift as a guard at the Dravo boat yard, he left the house by three in the afternoon for a workday that ended at midnight. After an abbreviated night's sleep, Dad would start his never-ending cup of coffee, have a few Pall Malls and begin his labor of love. He wore guard clothes that had become too shabby for regular work wear: heavy black trousers, plain-toed black shoes and a gray shirt that my mother no longer ironed crisp and that no longer had the benefit of the thin metal collar stay. He did not shave till it was time to go to the boat yard, and so he often had a day's growth or more.

Dad's labors went on for longer periods of time as Christmas drew near. During the last several days, he would extend these efforts, sometimes working all night, finding his rest for the next boat yard shift in a nap. His work coupled with my mother's flurry of activities: Shopping and baking and decorating created much of the holiday excitement. There was about the house a quickened pace, a Saturday morning sense— the opposite of Sunday afternoon foreboding—that signaled coming joy. It was now everywhere, every day, all day long.

One of the most difficult parts of the waiting was not being able to go through the living room into the vestibule and up the stairs to Mar's, my name for Sophie, a word I couldn't pronounce (we called John Marmak "Daddy Mar"). We would have to go through the basement, taking a circuitous route that ended in a dark, drafty hall leading to her living room. And we had to go because Mar's was our second home. Their living room was where the other parts of Christmas happened. Though not as secretive as my father, Mar would spend hours decorating her mantel. She would cover the wall above it with wrapping paper and tiny lights that spelled Noel or Merry Xmas, and she would line the mantel with little winter figurines and a crèche in a field of cotton snow.

We also went there for the vegetable beef soup Daddy Mar cooked on Saturdays. It was his own recipe and he would make enough for the entire week. Each day he would warm some for his supper and add it to noodles that were kept in a separate bowl, also cooked on the weekend. The soup was special, so much so that my brother, who didn't like carrots, would eat them only in Daddy Mar's recipe. We usually had at least one bowl at the kitchen table on every visit, regardless the time of day. But at Christmas, Mar would let us eat in the living room. First she would spread newspaper on the floor and then bring in the soup with either slices of Mayflower's rye bread with chunks of butter or a ham sandwich and a tall glass of iced tea with a piece of lemon.
And we would watch the marionettes in *The Night Before Christmas* and *The First Christmas*. There on the floor of her living room we would wait for Christmas.

Sleep was difficult. It seemed to come just before we were awakened. As Mickey and I stood in our sleeper pajamas with the soled feet, I almost didn't want the doors to open. Waiting had taken on a life of its own and in the wait a new meaning had come to be. In the wait was a life where all possibilities existed; once the doors were opened, the anticipation would end. In its place came wonder and excitement.

There was so much to see and take in. There, just beyond the doors, was a city. A city that stretched all the way to the windows across the room. The streets were made of white sand, edged by the green sand of the yards where the houses with their cellophane windows, many built of wood by Dad's own hands, sat next to the latest Plasticville buildings: the hospital, the diner and the split-levels. The street lights were hand-bent, each with its own tiny bulb, and stood near to telephone poles as hand-painted citizens made their way motionlessly along the streets.

There were two Lionel trains: the Santa Fe, with its imaginary passengers eating and sleeping and enjoying the winter scene, and a freight train complete with a log-dumping car and a smoke-puffing engine. The city had an industrial section and a downtown and a poor section, all neat and near to one another. On the two ends of the platform were elevated sections: one held the airport and Dad's handmade mountains, and the other, across the room near the windows, held the Christmas tree topped with an angel. Beneath the tree sat the manger, the reason for it all, according to what we learned each day at St. Francis De Sales school.

While that was also part of Dad's reason for this creation, I believe his real motivation was to let the three of us know how important we were to him. And so he would give us this world, his world, each Christmas.

I left McKees Rocks nearly 50 years ago. And yet each Christmas season, as I prepare for the holidays, I open my box of Christmas memories. This one is always there, a lasting treasure.